DISCOVER DG GRAPHICS

THE
BROTHERS
A HMONG GRAPHIC FOLKTALE

BY SHEELUE YANG
ILLUSTRATED BY LE NHAT VU

PICTURE WINDOW BOOKS
a capstone imprint

Published by Picture Window Books, an imprint of Capstone.
1710 Roe Crest Drive, North Mankato, Minnesota 56003
capstonepub.com

Library of Congress Cataloging-in-Publication Data is available on the Library of Congress website.

ISBN: 9781484672334 (hardcover)
ISBN: 9781484672938 (paperback)
ISBN: 9781484672945 (ebook PDF)

Summary: In this Hmong folktale, two brothers venture into a remote jungle, hunting food for their hungry family. But the jungle is full of dangerous wild animals. The older brother vows to keep his younger brother safe . . . or die trying.

Designed by Kay Fraser

Author's Note:
The Hmong have preserved our history through oral stories, passed down from parent to child over generations. These stories are often tragic and fantastic: animals speak and become companions, children are orphaned and become princes and princesses beyond the clouds, siblings are separated and born again as neighboring trees. In Hmong folktales, we are introduced to different worlds that coexist and function as a single landscape. This story is a tale of brotherly love, a reminder of the power of the animals in the wild, and the bonds that keep us together.

Printed in the United States 5395

CAST OF CHARACTERS

Tou Dao is the older brother of Tou Ger. He is an expert archer and brave hunter.

Tou Ger is the younger brother of Tou Dao. He learns the ways of the jungle from his older brother.

The Buffalos are a gentle herd of water buffalos. They want to protect Tou Dao and Tou Ger.

HOW TO READ A GRAPHIC NOVEL

Graphic novels are easy to read. Boxes called panels show you how to follow the story. Look at the panels from left to right and top to bottom.

Read the word boxes and word balloons from left to right as well. Don't forget the sound and action words in the pictures.

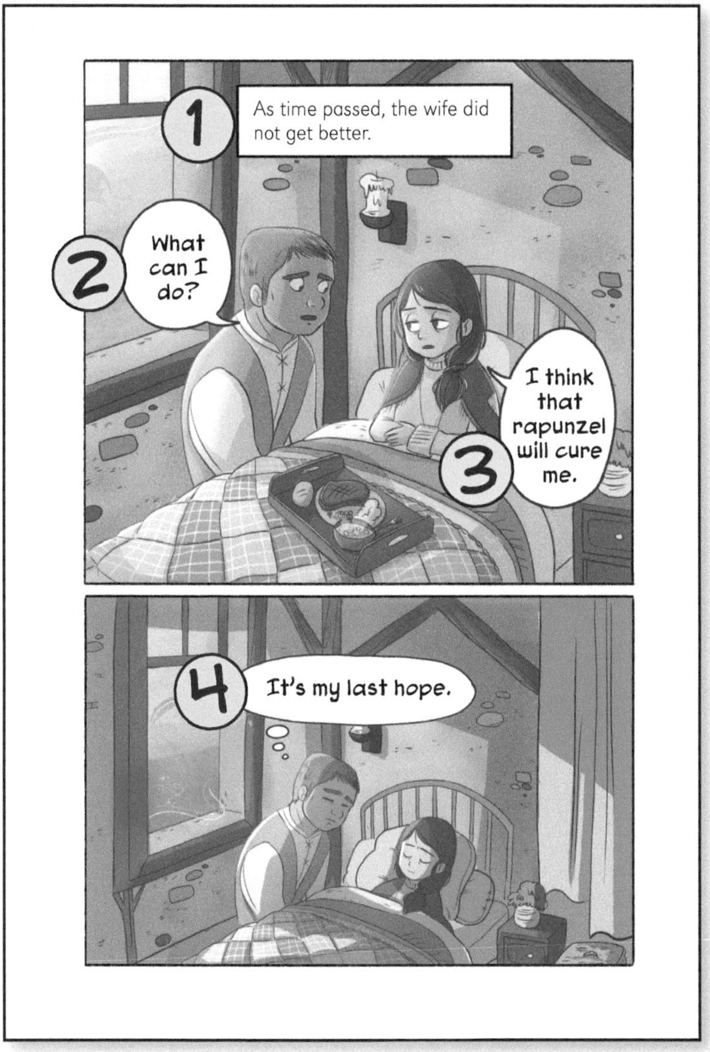
1
As time passed, the wife did not get better.
2
What can I do?
3
I think that rapunzel will cure me.
4
It's my last hope.

The pictures and the words work together to tell the whole story.

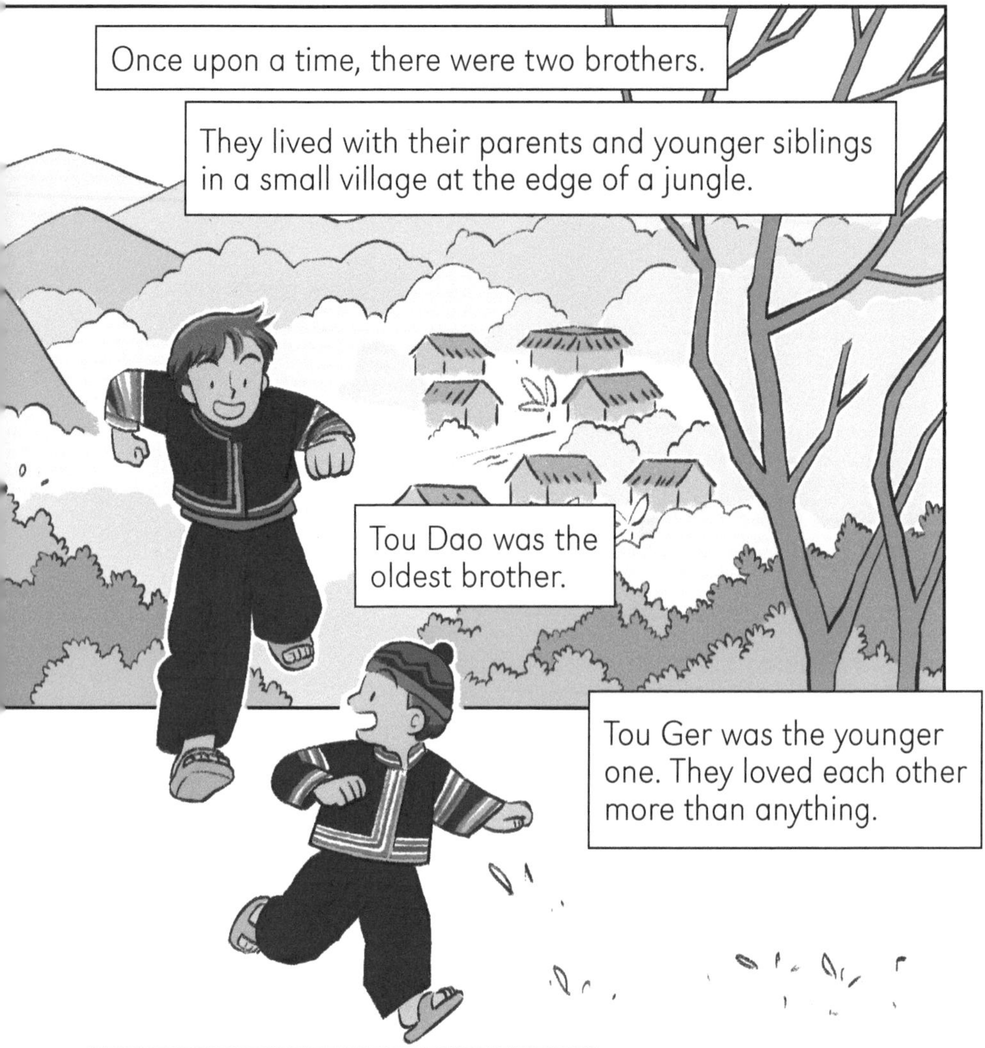
Once upon a time, there were two brothers.
They lived with their parents and younger siblings in a small village at the edge of a jungle.
Tou Dao was the oldest brother.
Tou Ger was the younger one. They loved each other more than anything.

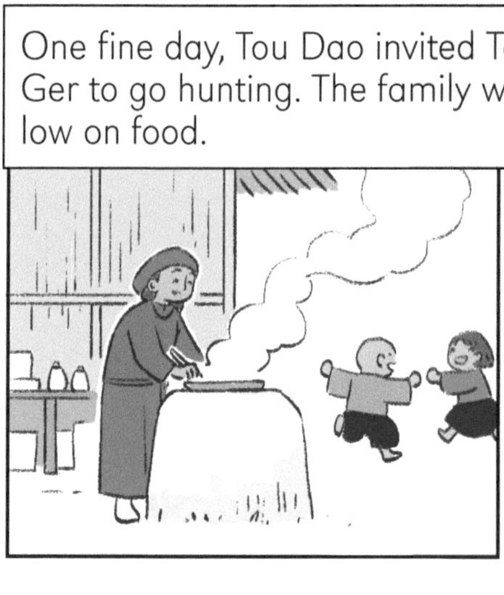
One fine day, Tou Dao invited Tou Ger to go hunting. The family was low on food.

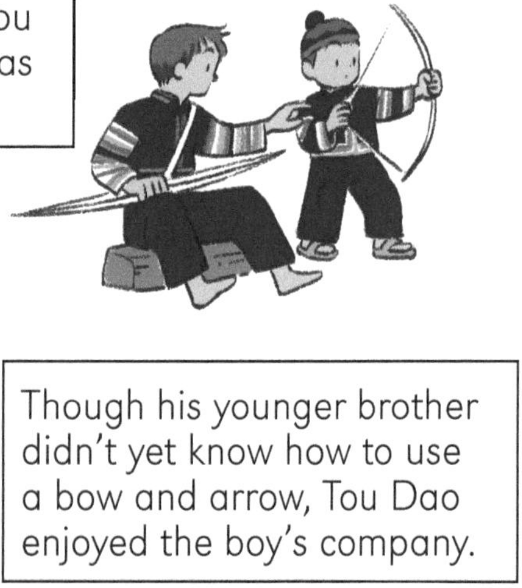
Though his younger brother didn't yet know how to use a bow and arrow, Tou Dao enjoyed the boy's company.

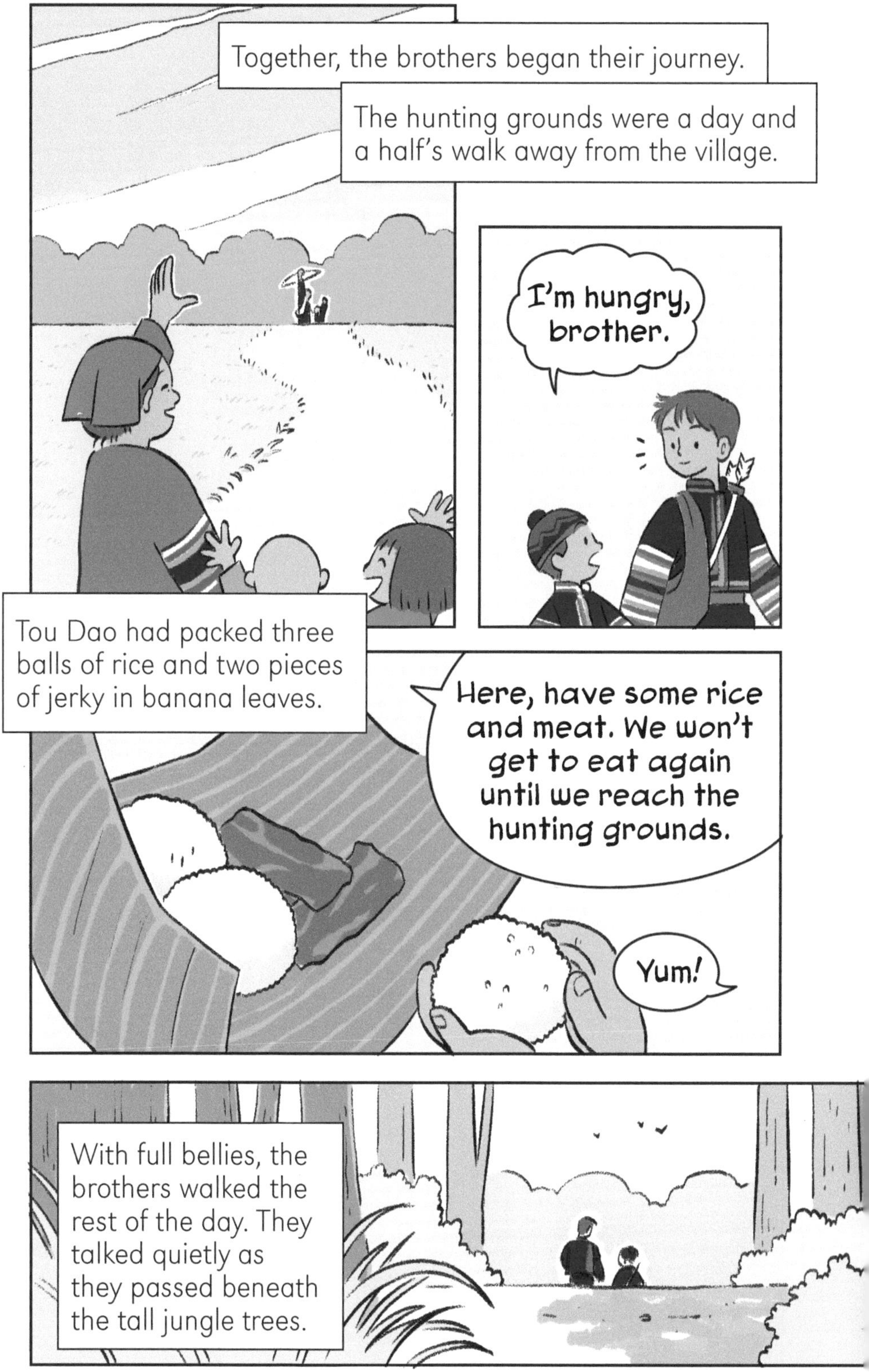
Together, the brothers began their journey.
The hunting grounds were a day and a half's walk away from the village.
I'm hungry, brother.
Tou Dao had packed three balls of rice and two pieces of jerky in banana leaves.
Here, have some rice and meat. We won't get to eat again until we reach the hunting grounds.
Yum!
With full bellies, the brothers walked the rest of the day. They talked quietly as they passed beneath the tall jungle trees.

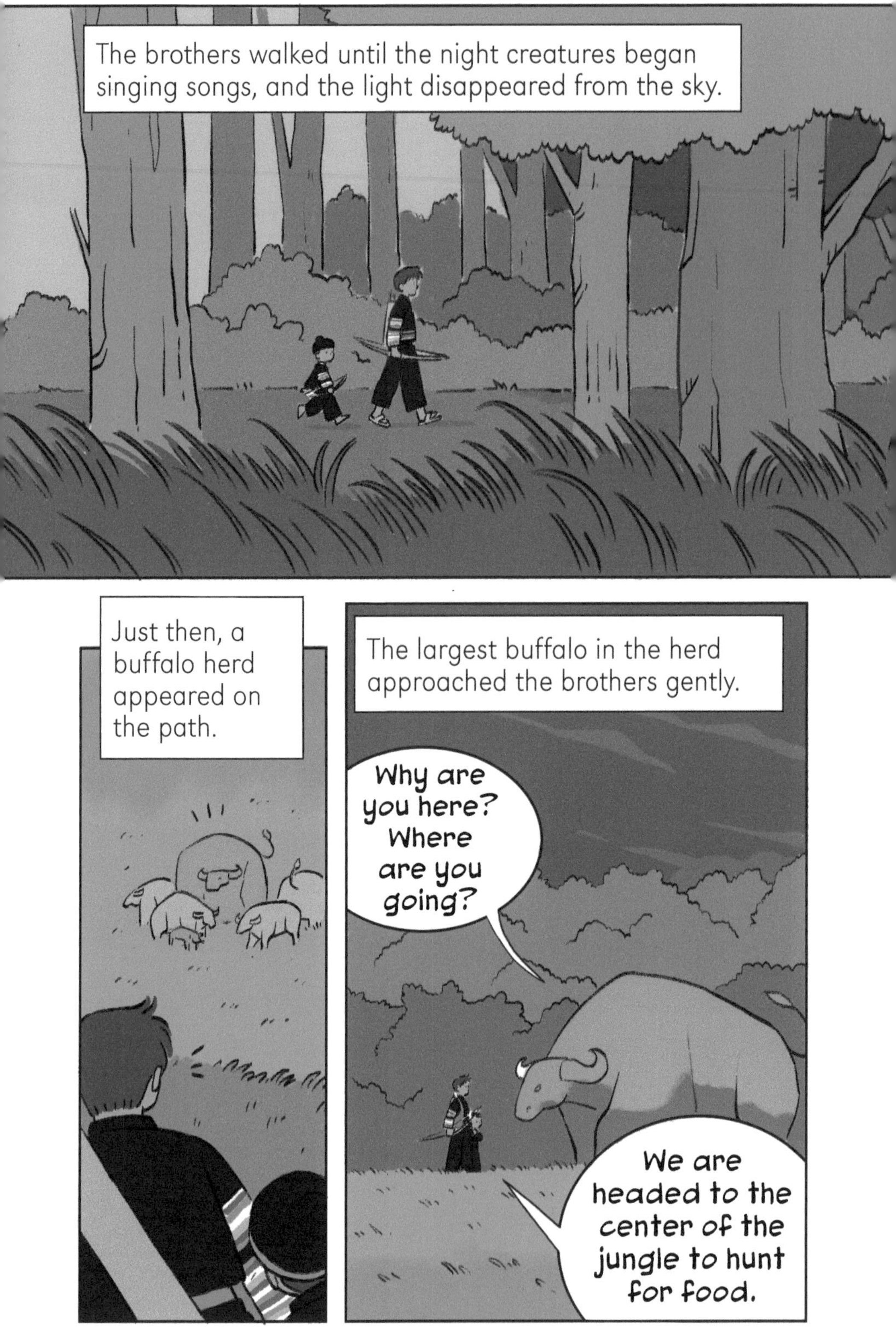
The brothers walked until the night creatures began singing songs, and the light disappeared from the sky.
Just then, a buffalo herd appeared on the path.
The largest buffalo in the herd approached the brothers gently.
Why are you here? Where are you going?
We are headed to the center of the jungle to hunt for food.

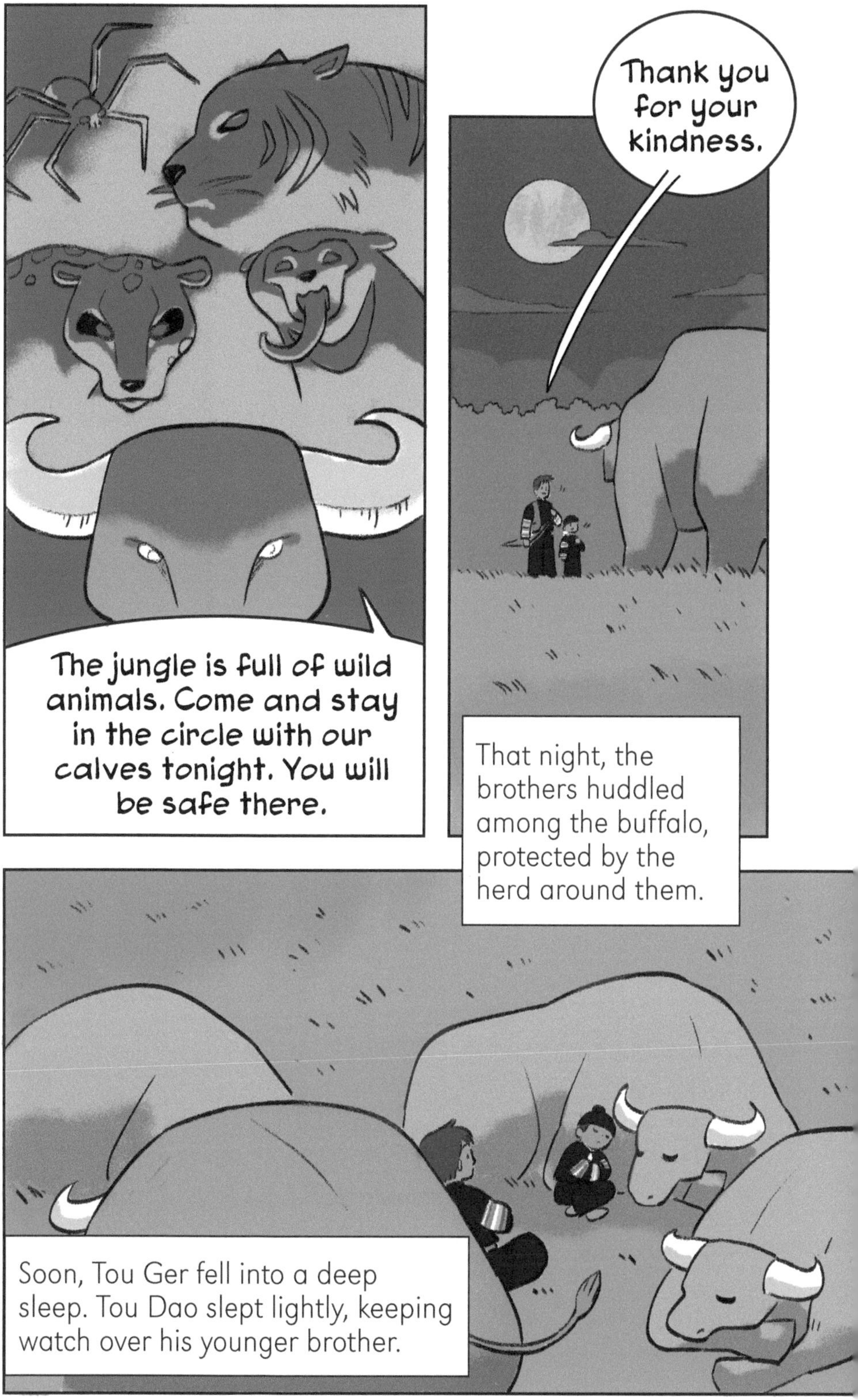

The jungle is full of wild animals. Come and stay in the circle with our calves tonight. You will be safe there.
Thank you for your kindness.
That night, the brothers huddled among the buffalo, protected by the herd around them.
Soon, Tou Ger fell into a deep sleep. Tou Dao slept lightly, keeping watch over his younger brother.

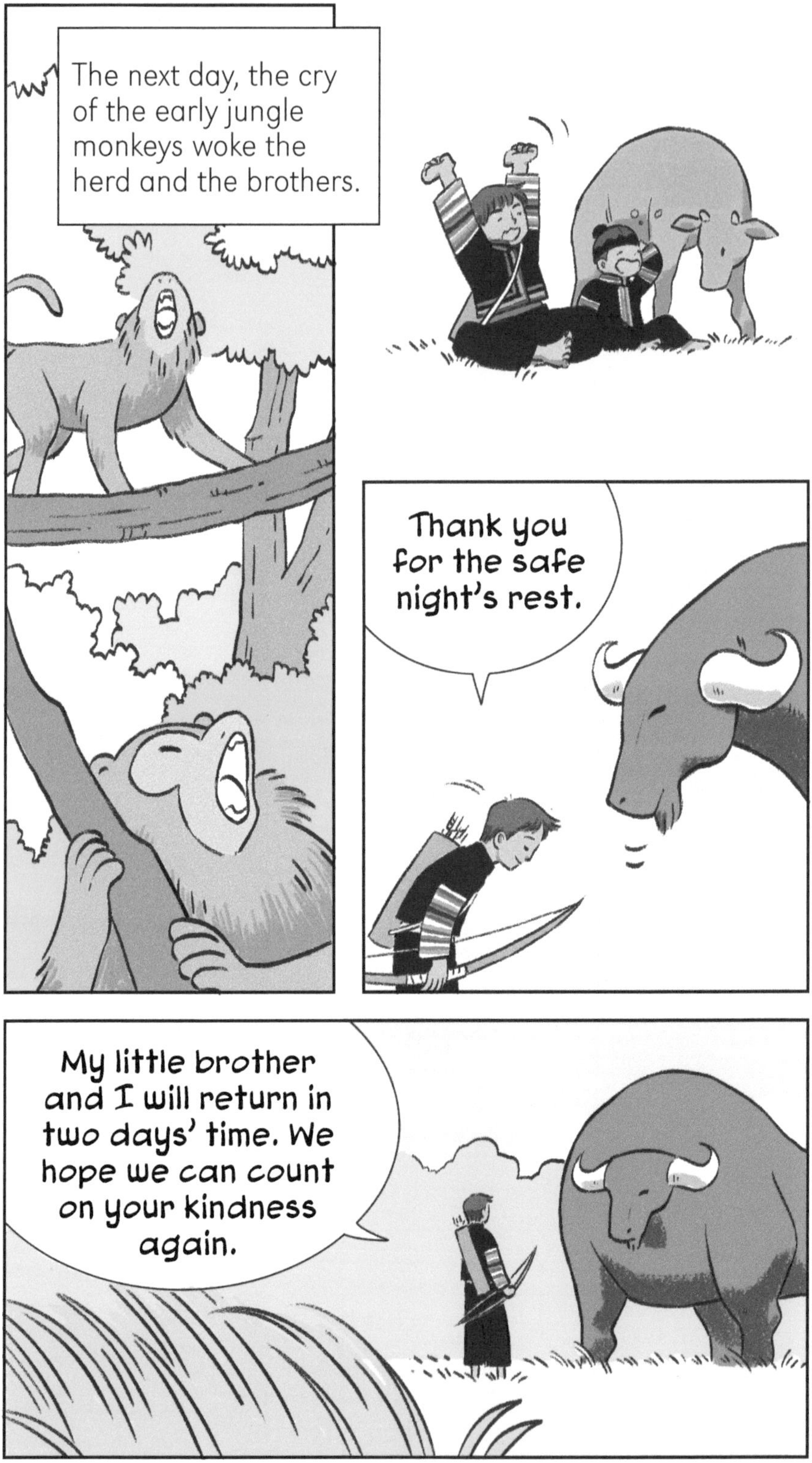
The next day, the cry of the early jungle monkeys woke the herd and the brothers.
Thank you for the safe night's rest.
My little brother and I will return in two days' time. We hope we can count on your kindness again.

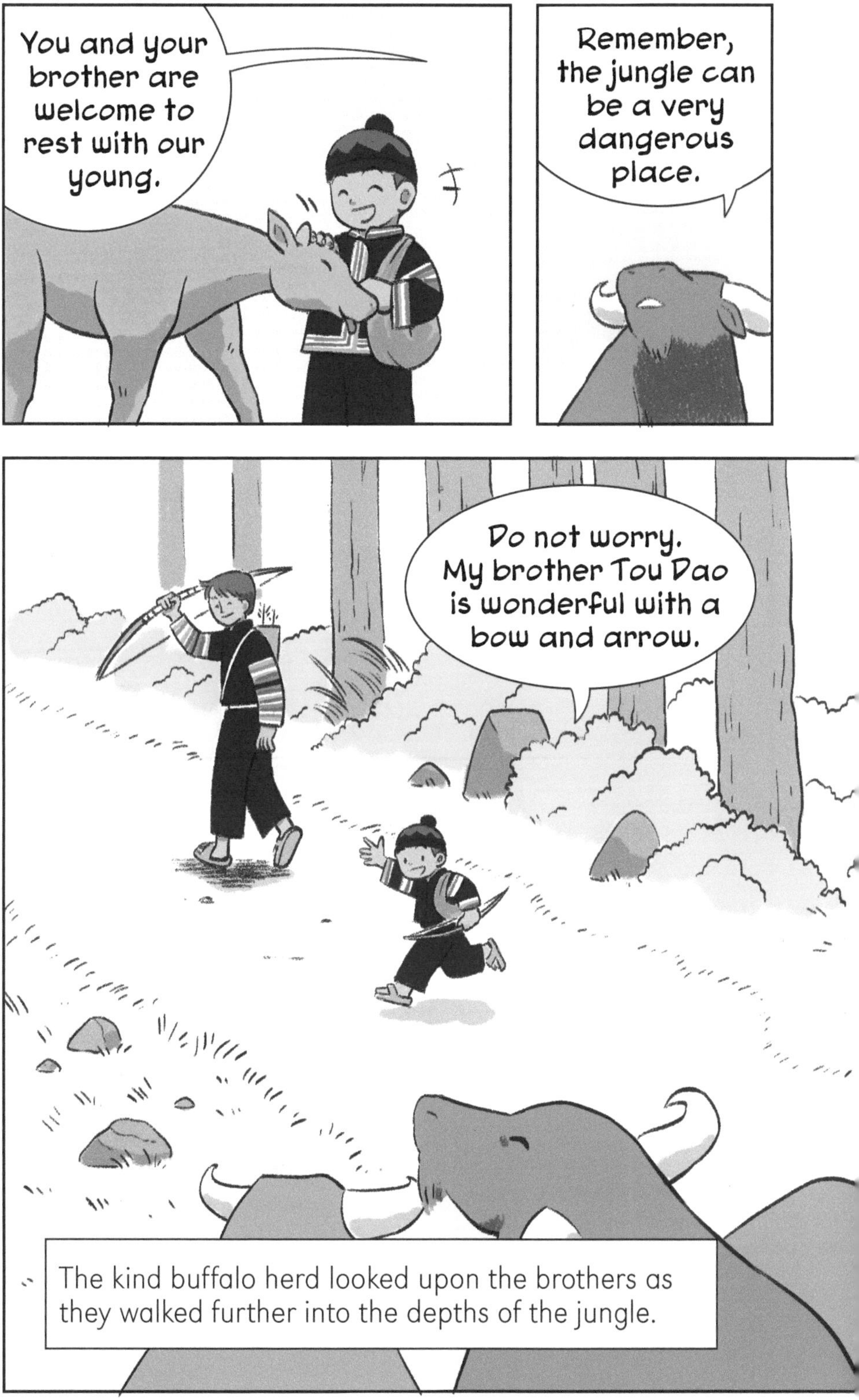
You and your brother are welcome to rest with our young.
Remember, the jungle can be a very dangerous place.
Do not worry. My brother Tou Dao is wonderful with a bow and arrow.
The kind buffalo herd looked upon the brothers as they walked further into the depths of the jungle.

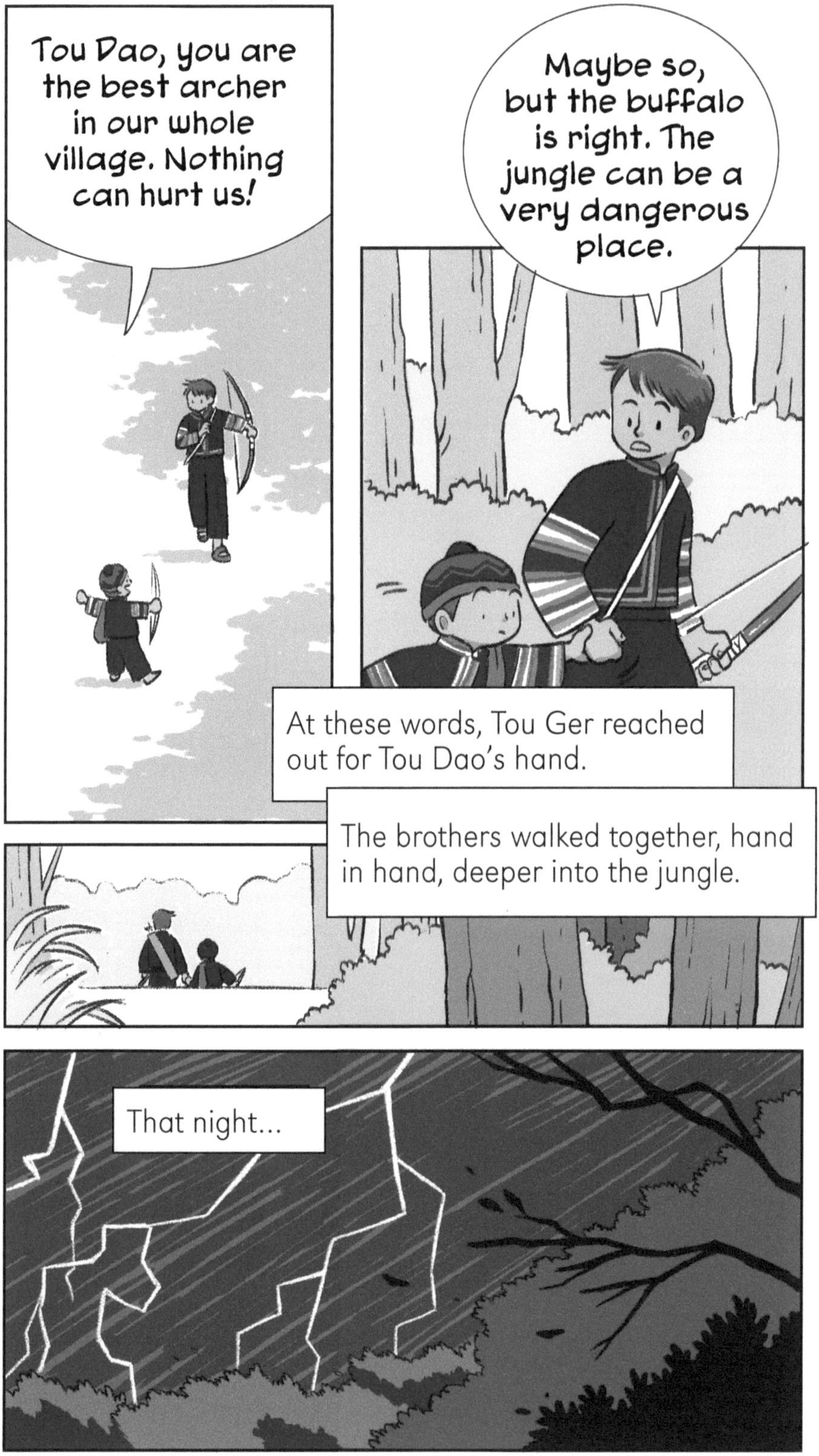
Tou Dao, you are the best archer in our whole village. Nothing can hurt us!
Maybe so, but the buffalo is right. The jungle can be a very dangerous place.
At these words, Tou Ger reached out for Tou Dao's hand.
The brothers walked together, hand in hand, deeper into the jungle.
That night...

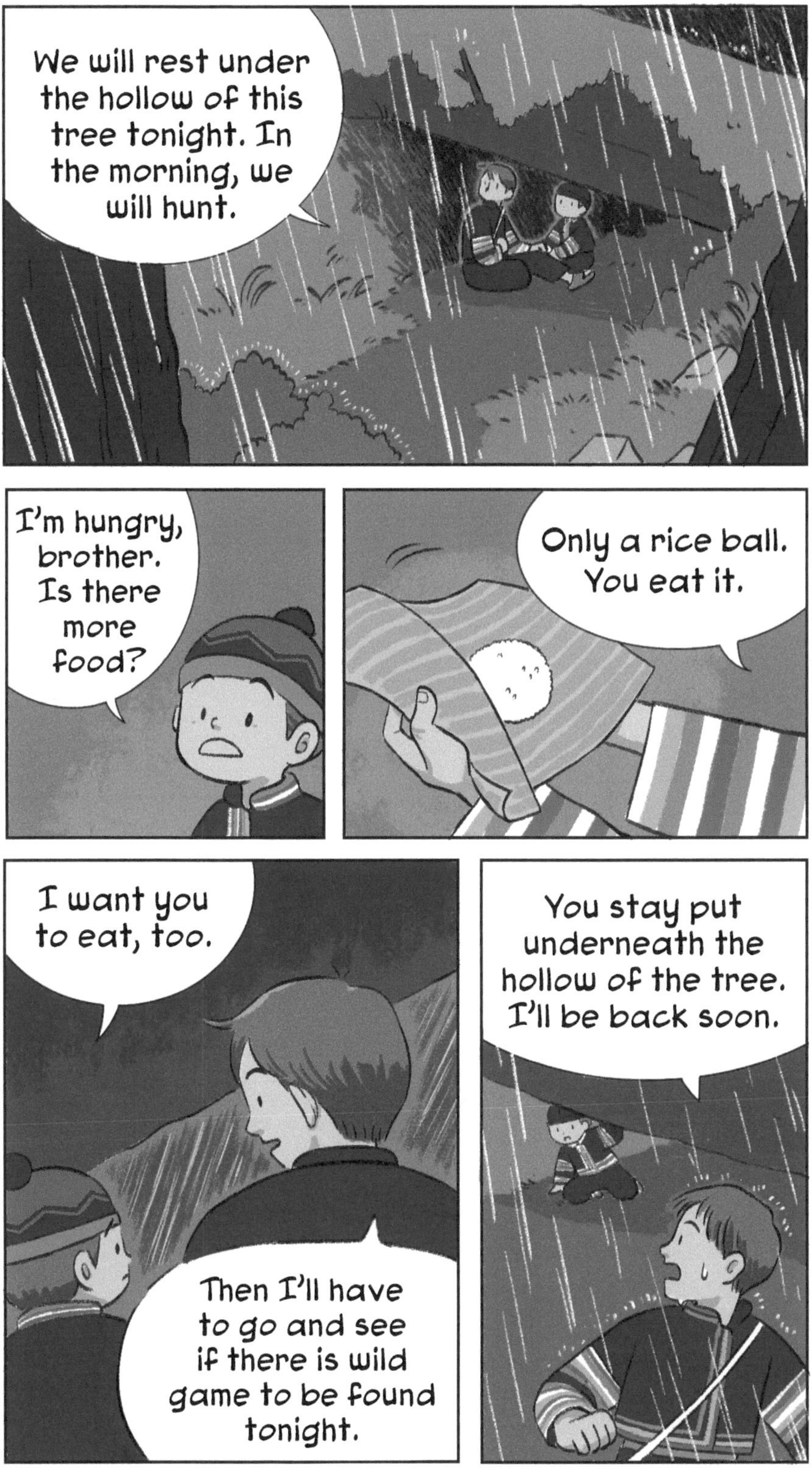
We will rest under the hollow of this tree tonight. In the morning, we will hunt.
I'm hungry, brother. Is there more food?
Only a rice ball. You eat it.
I want you to eat, too.
Then I'll have to go and see if there is wild game to be found tonight.
You stay put underneath the hollow of the tree. I'll be back soon.

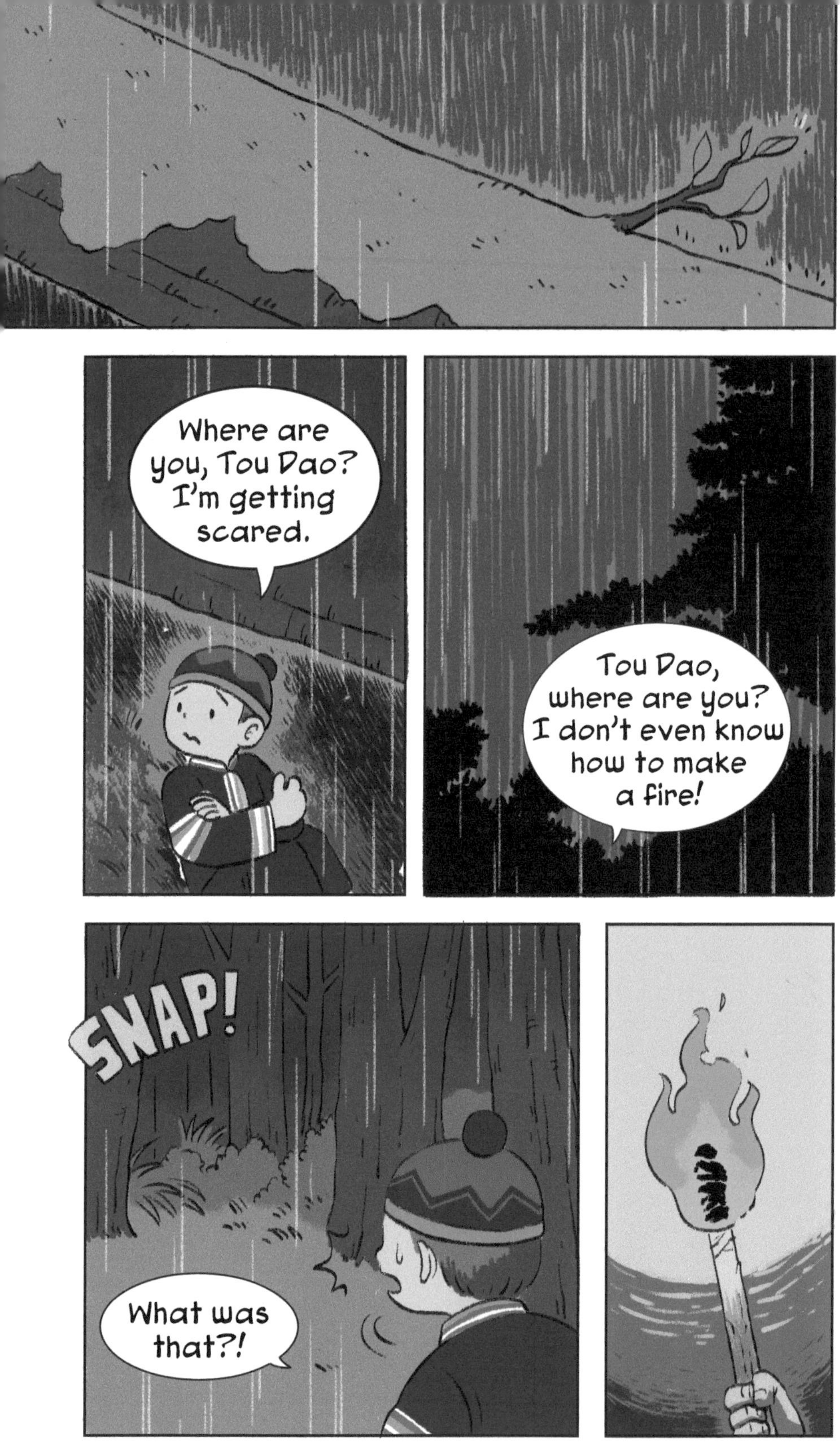
Where are you, Tou Dao? I'm getting scared.
Tou Dao, where are you? I don't even know how to make a fire!
SNAP!
What was that?!

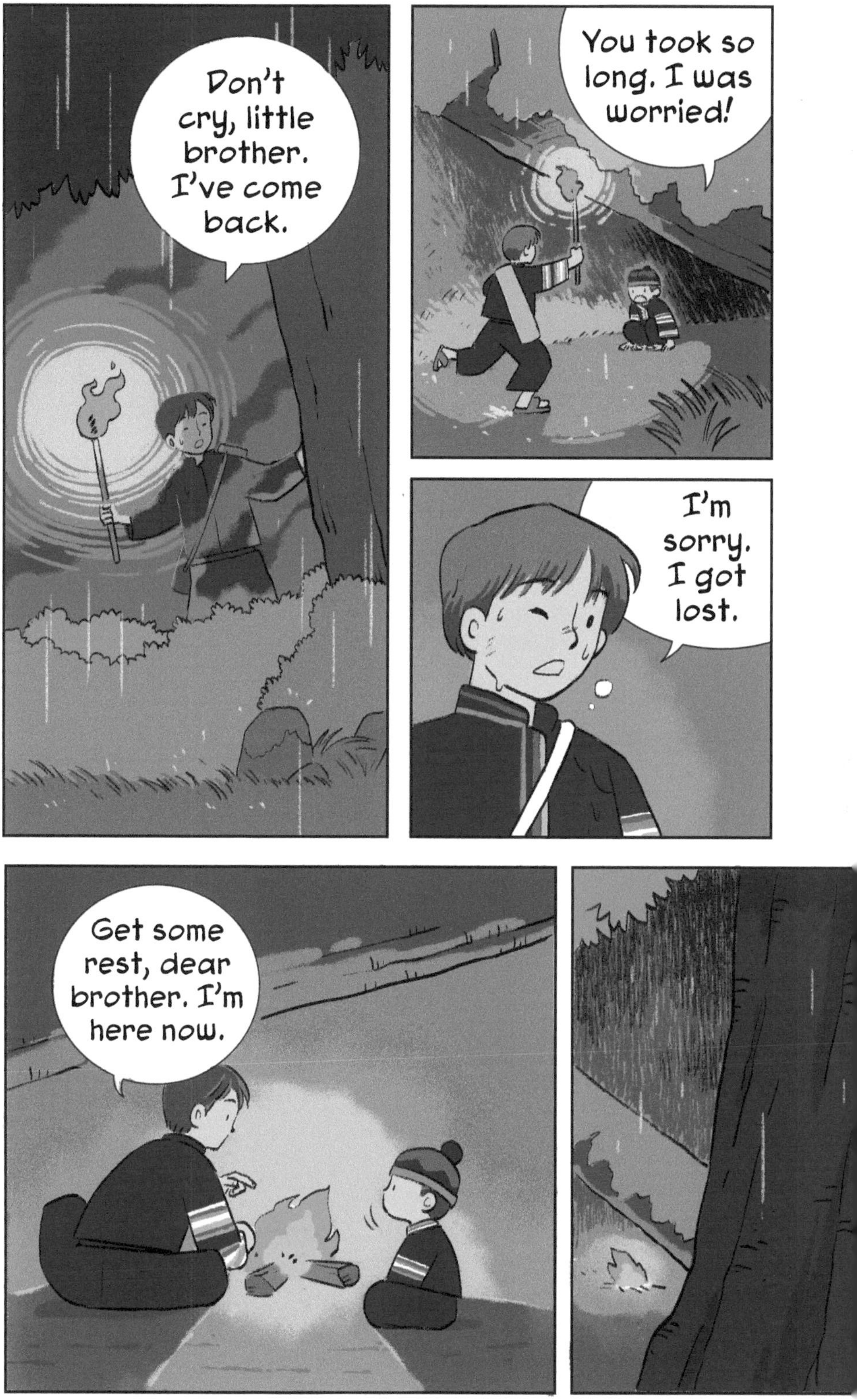
Don't cry, little brother. I've come back.
You took so long. I was worried!
I'm sorry. I got lost.
Get some rest, dear brother. I'm here now.

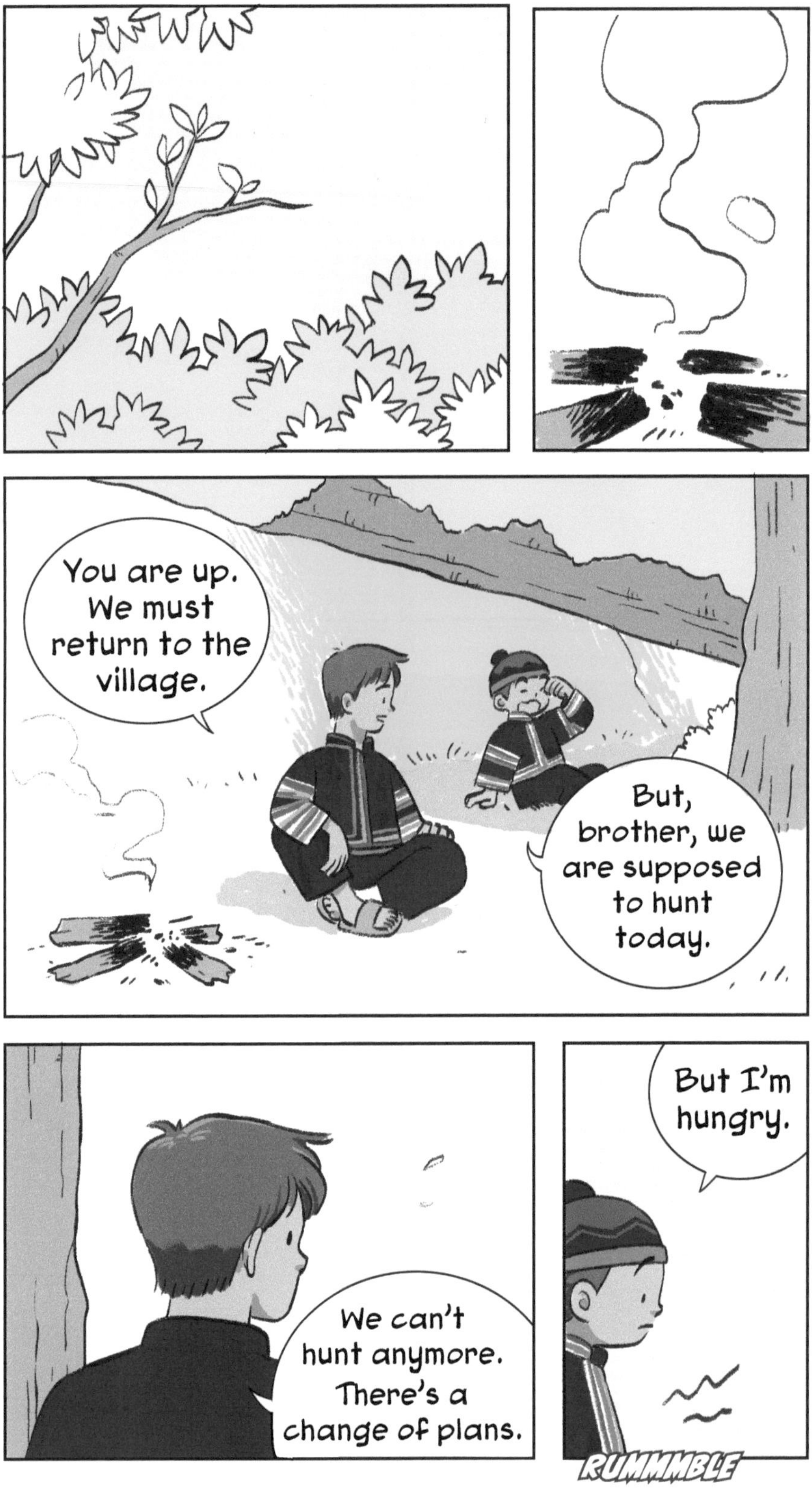
You are up. We must return to the village.
But, brother, we are supposed to hunt today.
We can't hunt anymore. There's a change of plans.
But I'm hungry.
RUMMMBLE

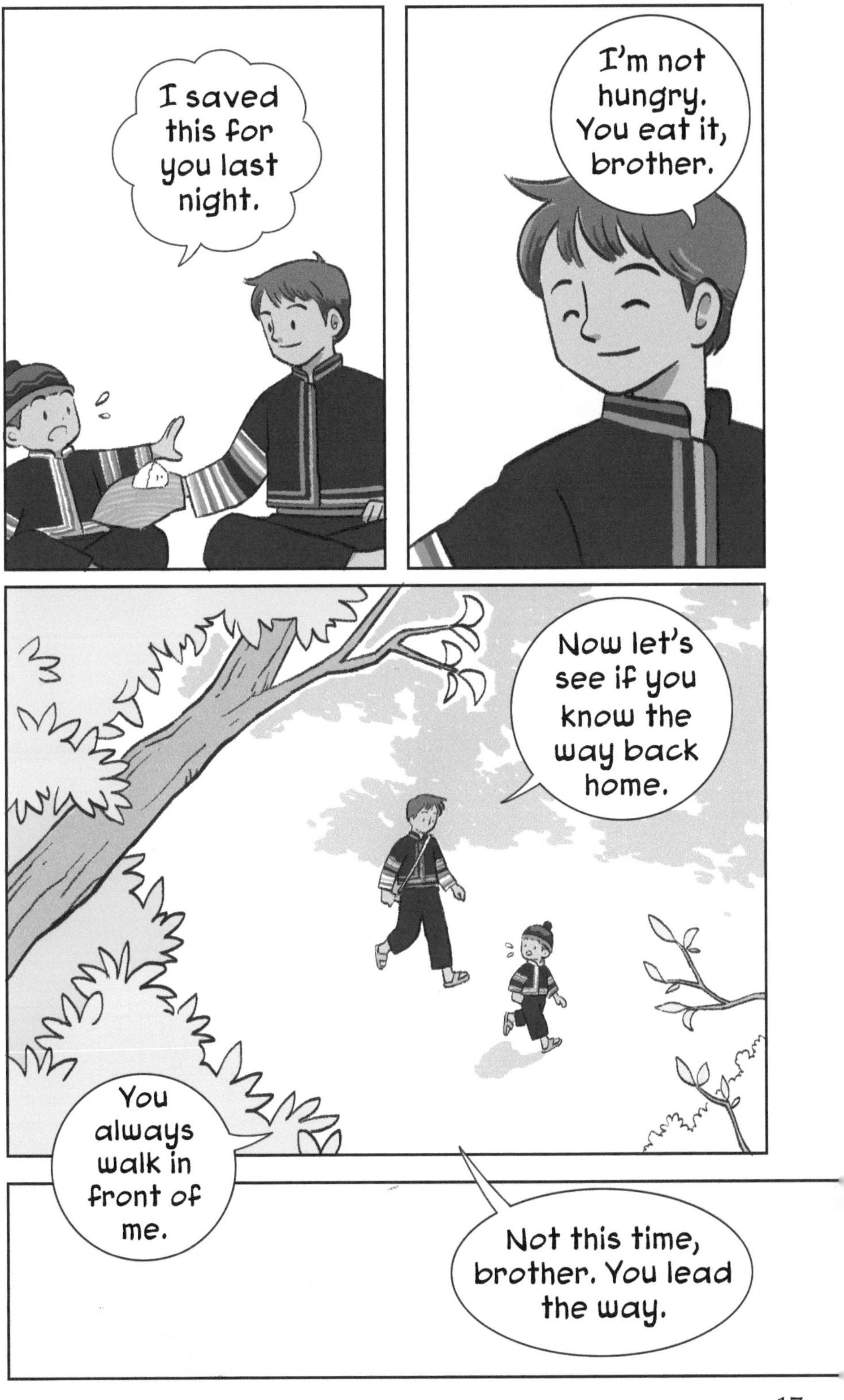
I saved this for you last night.
I'm not hungry. You eat it, brother.
Now let's see if you know the way back home.
You always walk in front of me.
Not this time, brother. You lead the way.

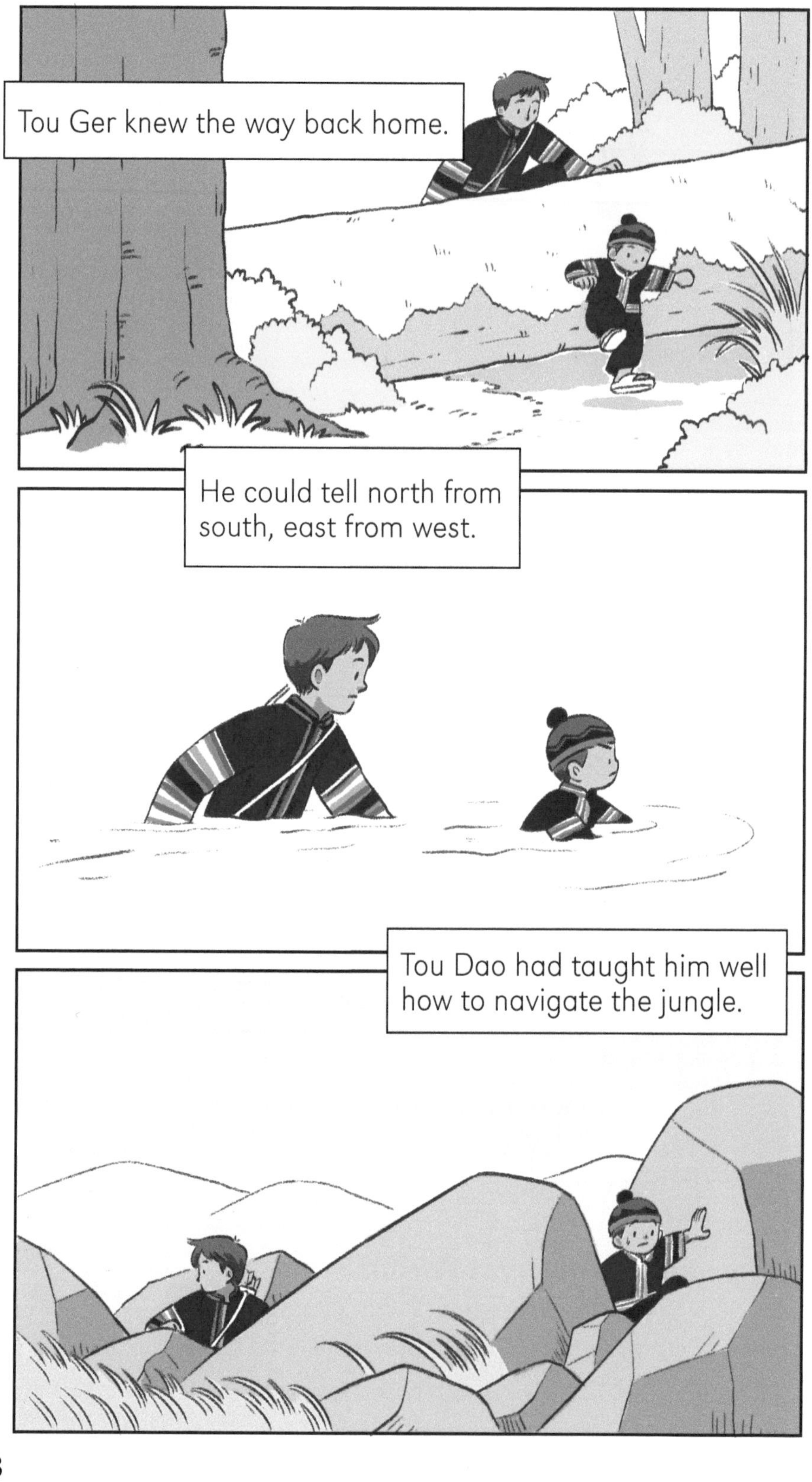
Tou Ger knew the way back home.
He could tell north from south, east from west.
Tou Dao had taught him well how to navigate the jungle.

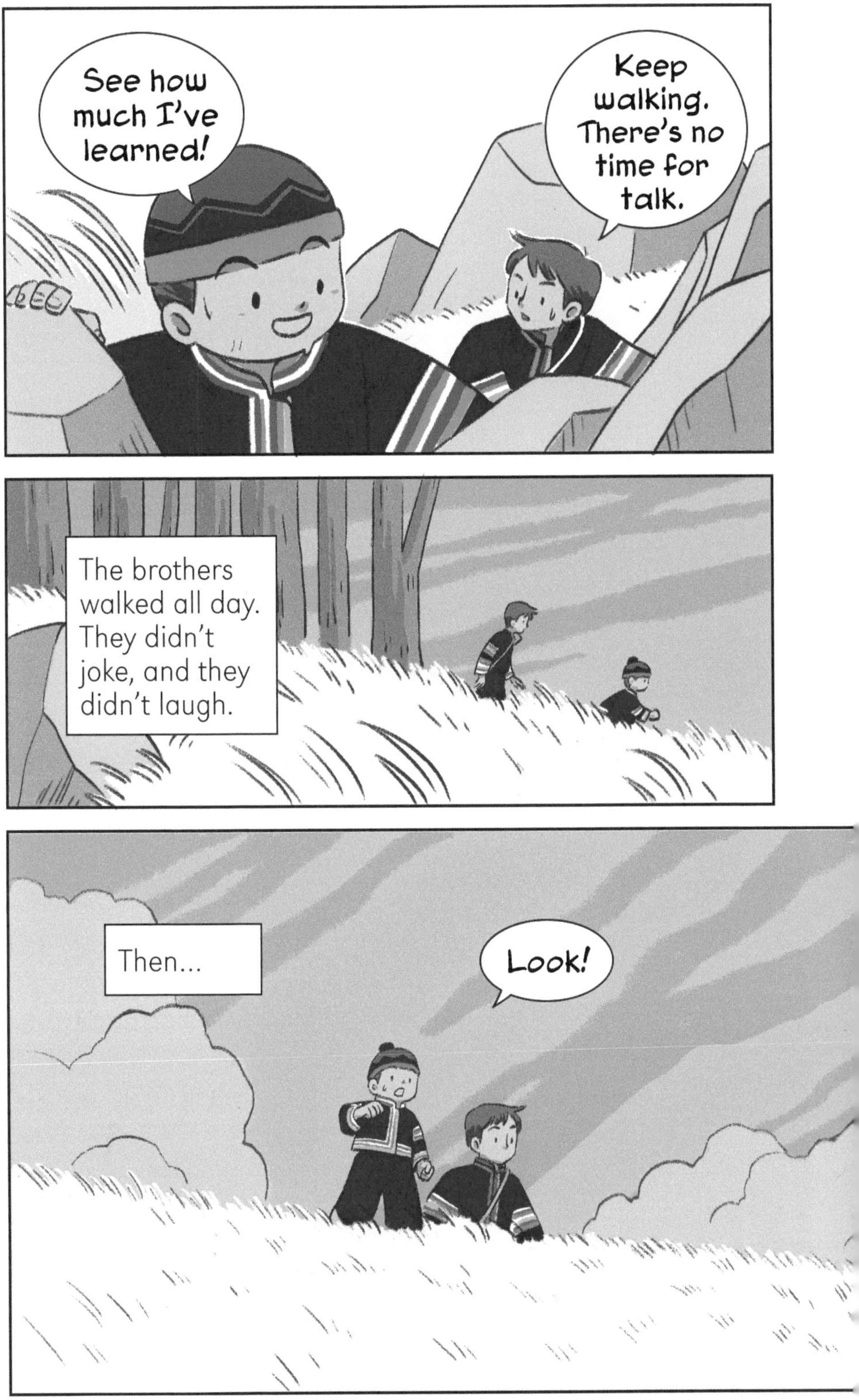
See how much I've learned!
Keep walking. There's no time for talk.
The brothers walked all day. They didn't joke, and they didn't laugh.
Then...
Look!

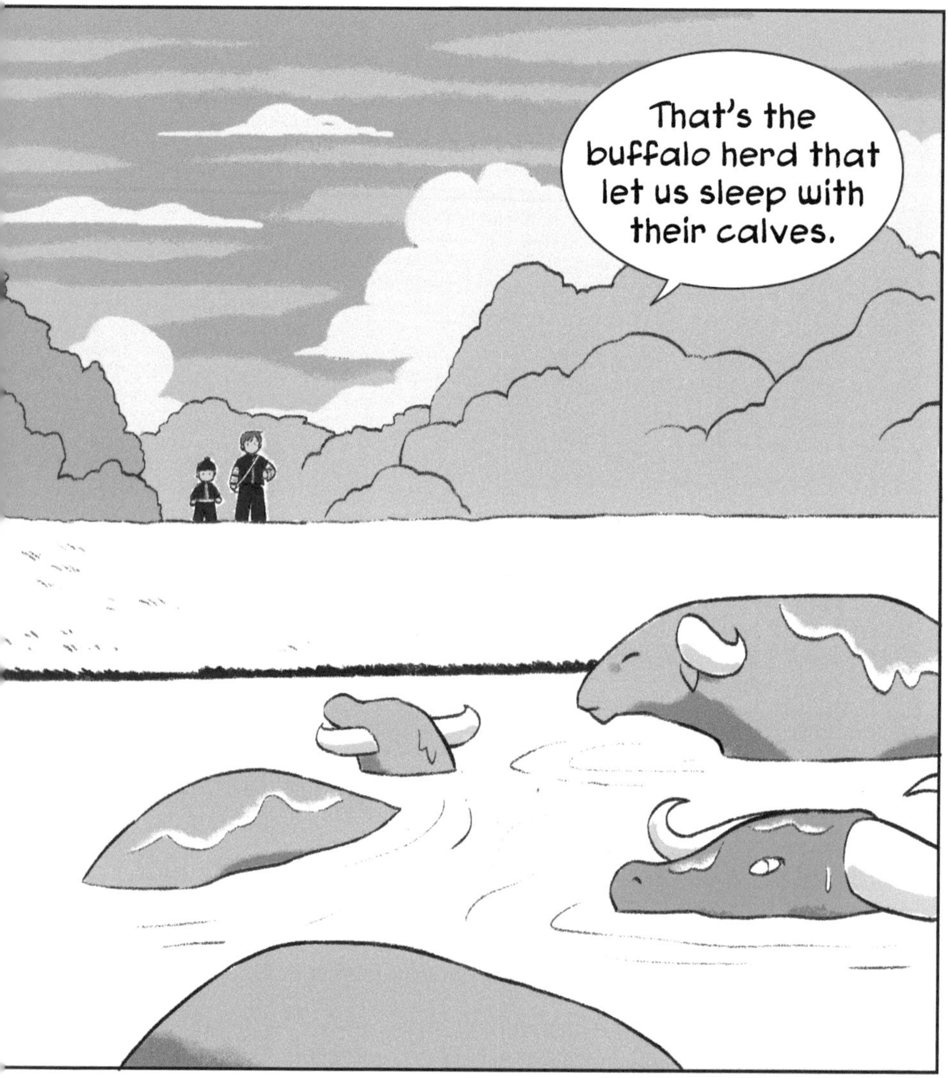
That's the buffalo herd that let us sleep with their calves.
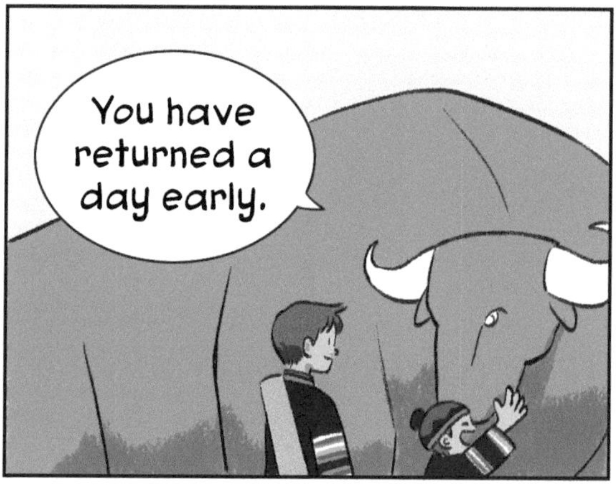
You have returned a day early.
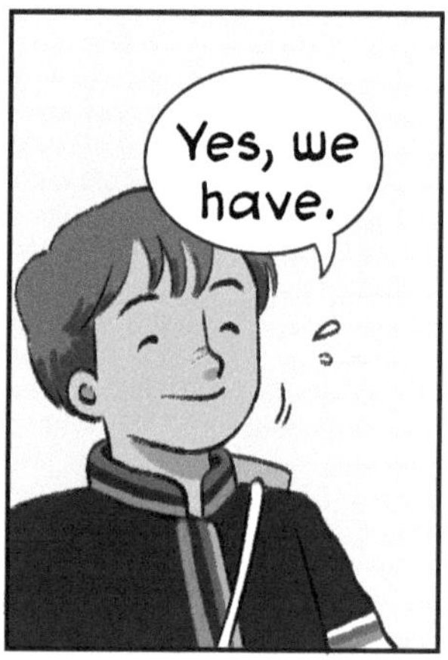
Yes, we have.

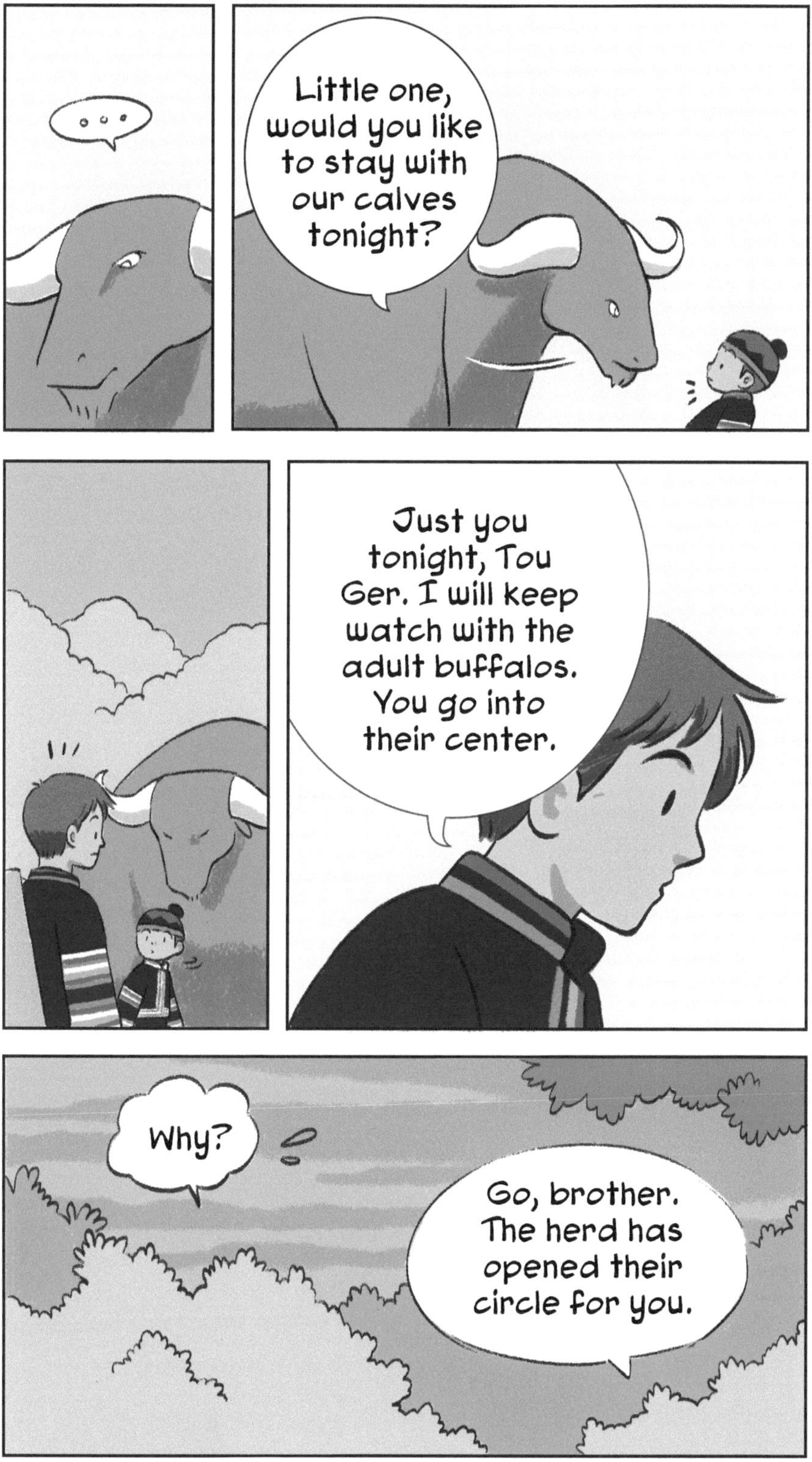
...
Little one, would you like to stay with our calves tonight?
Just you tonight, Tou Ger. I will keep watch with the adult buffalos. You go into their center.
Why?
Go, brother. The herd has opened their circle for you.

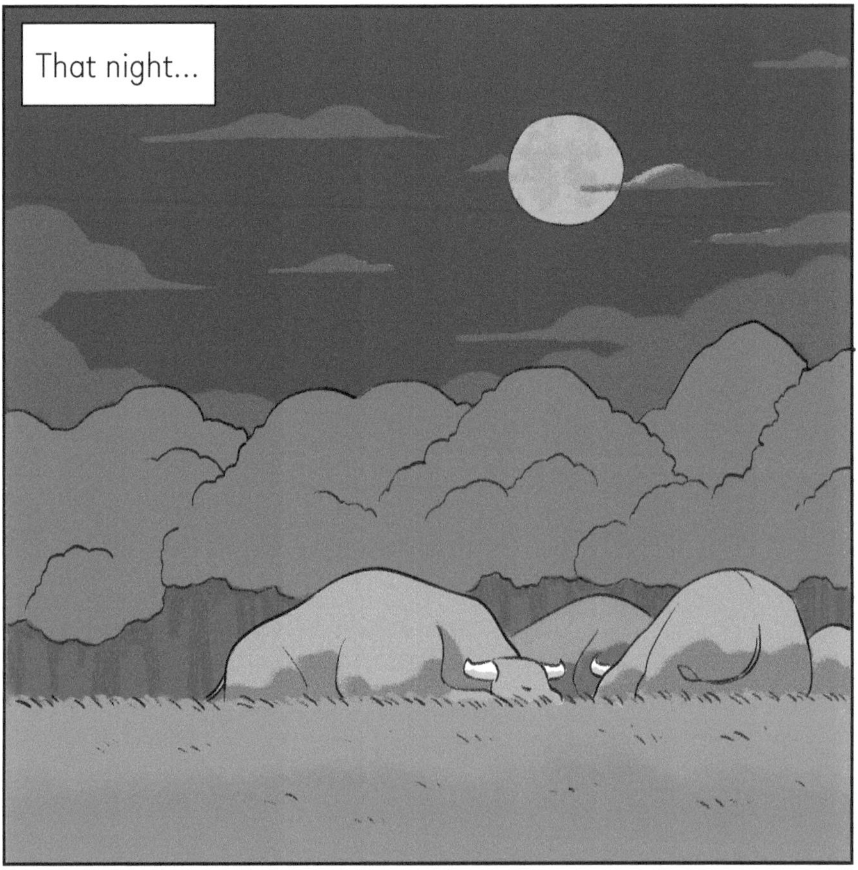
That night...

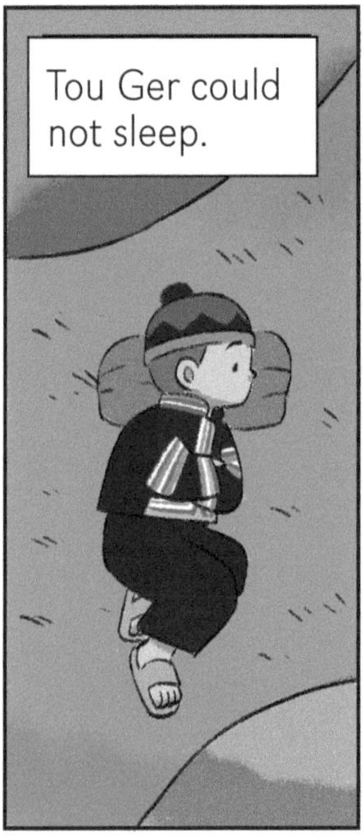
Tou Ger could not sleep.

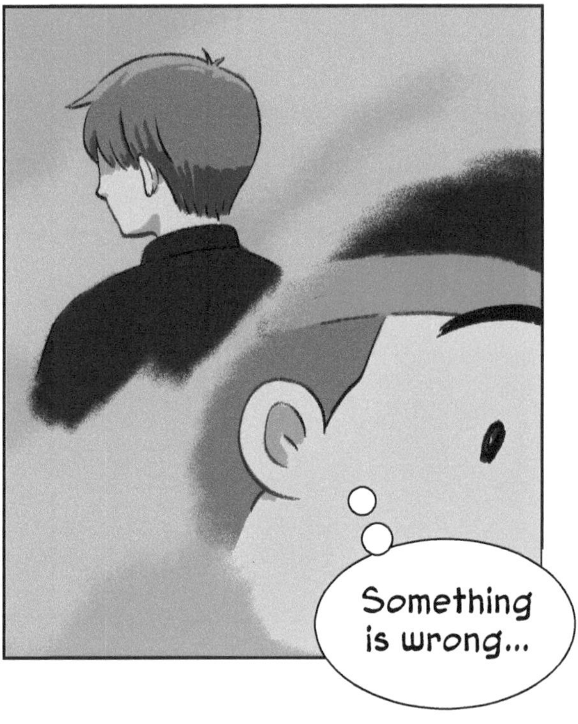
Something is wrong...

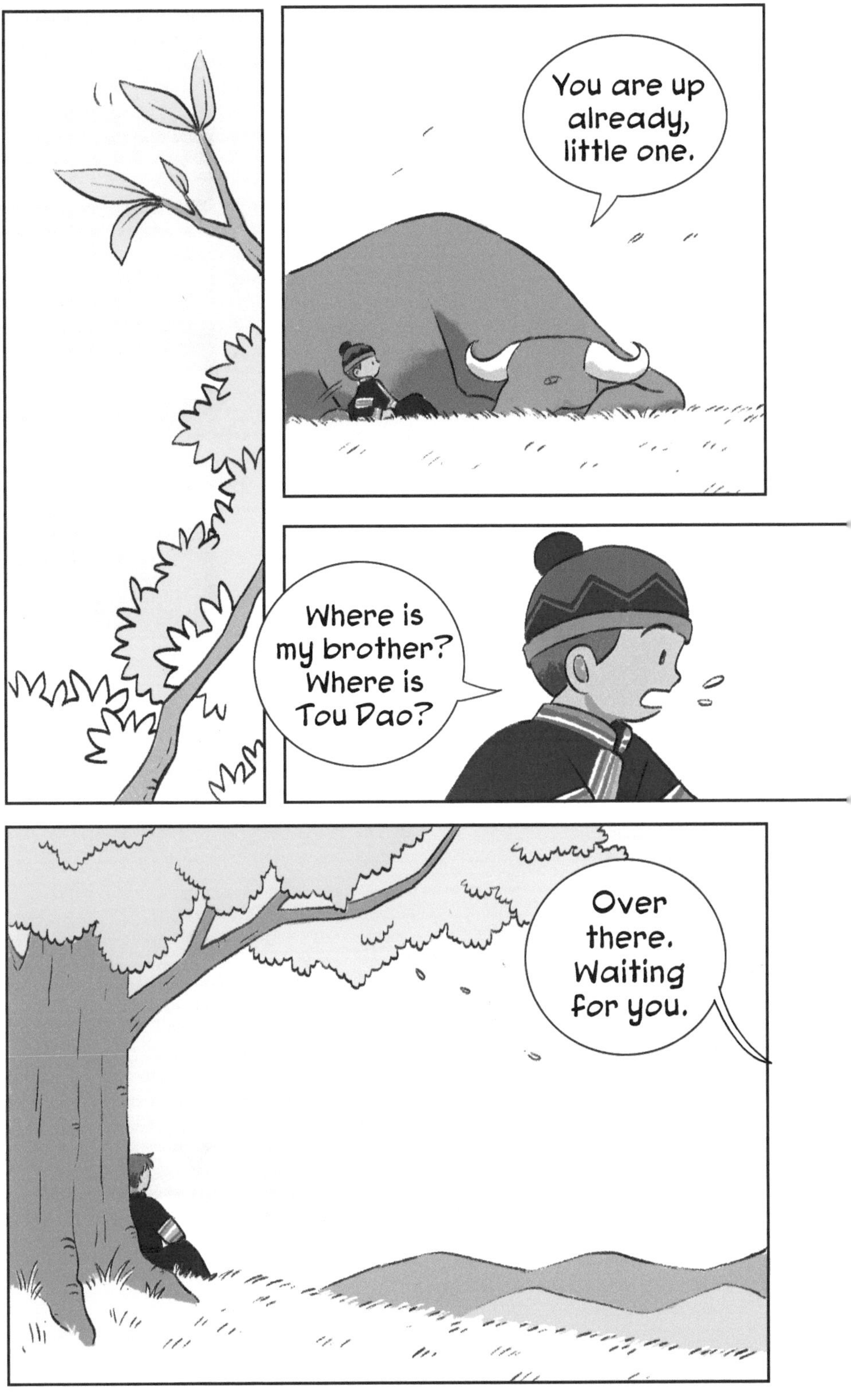
You are up already, little one.
Where is my brother? Where is Tou Dao?
Over there. Waiting for you.

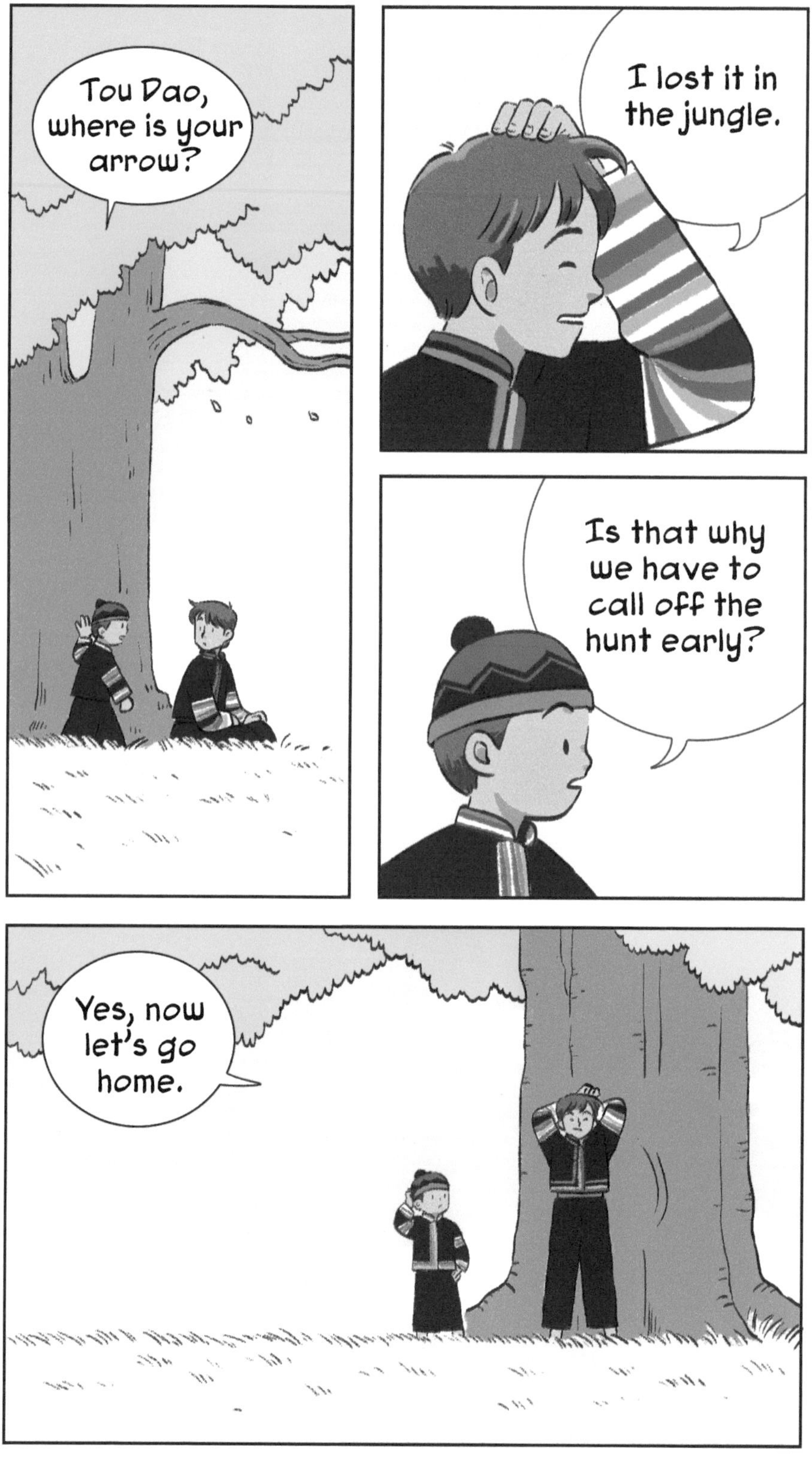
Tou Dao, where is your arrow?
I lost it in the jungle.
Is that why we have to call off the hunt early?
Yes, now let's go home.

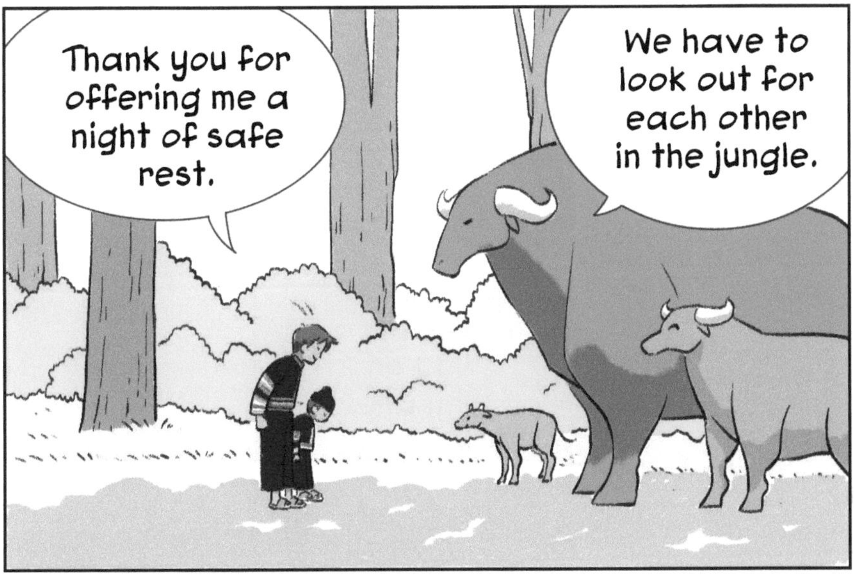
Thank you for offering me a night of safe rest.
We have to look out for each other in the jungle.

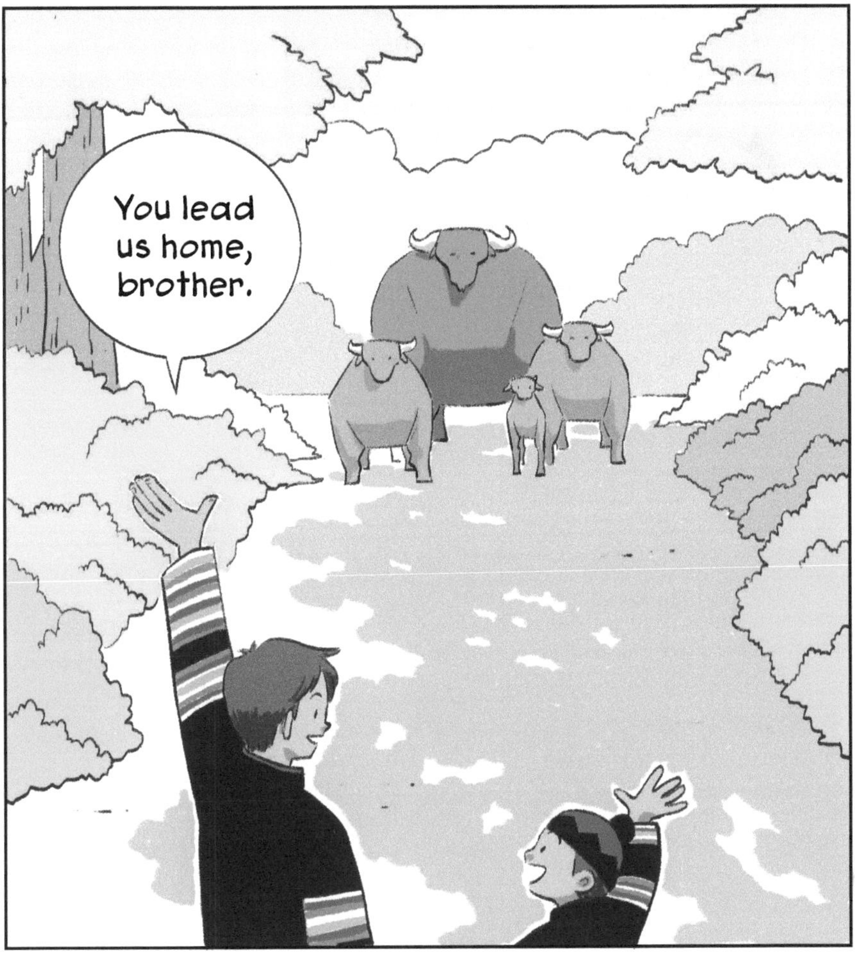
You lead us home, brother.

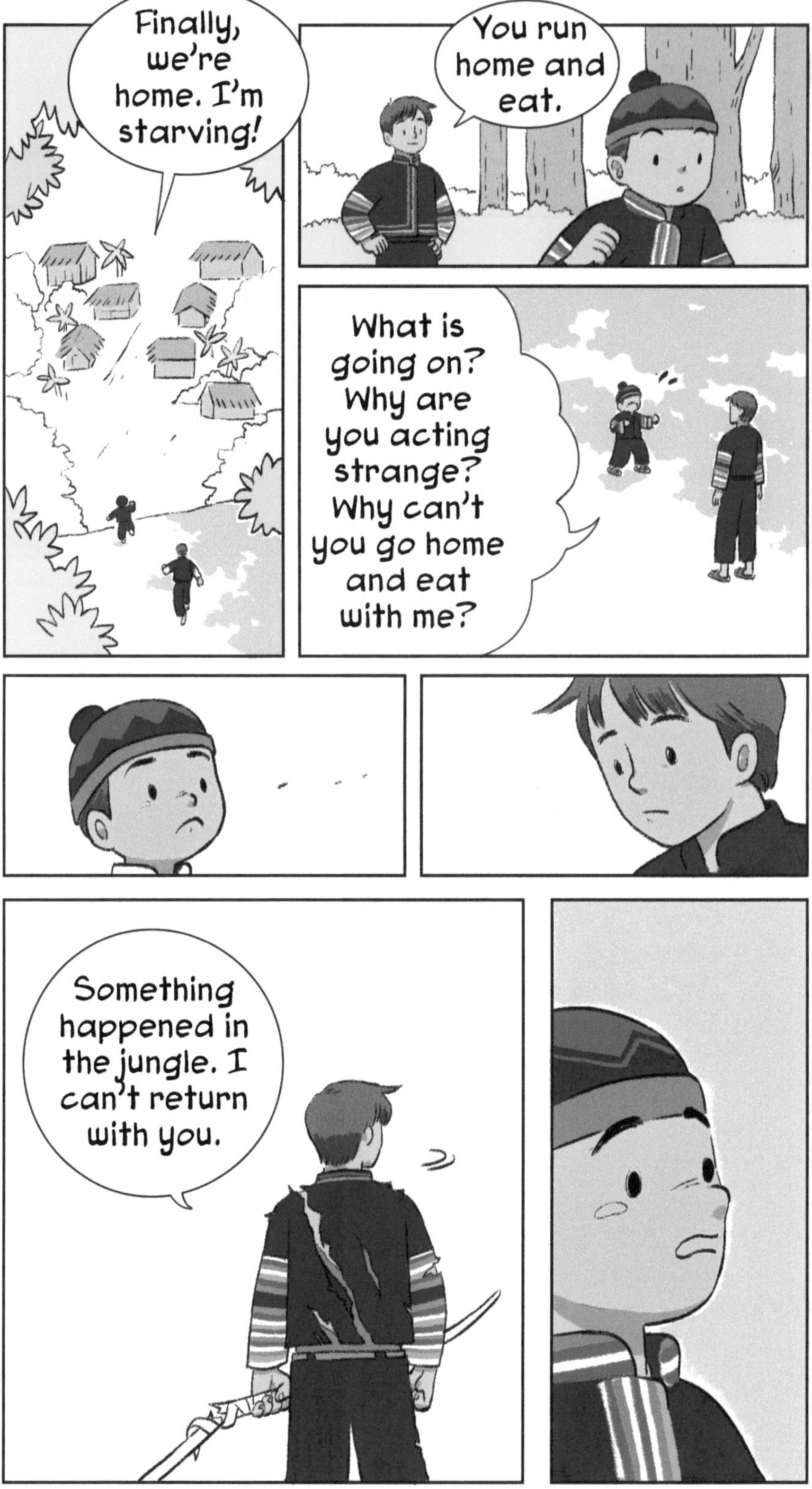
Finally, we're home. I'm starving!
You run home and eat.
What is going on? Why are you acting strange? Why can't you go home and eat with me?
Something happened in the jungle. I can't return with you.

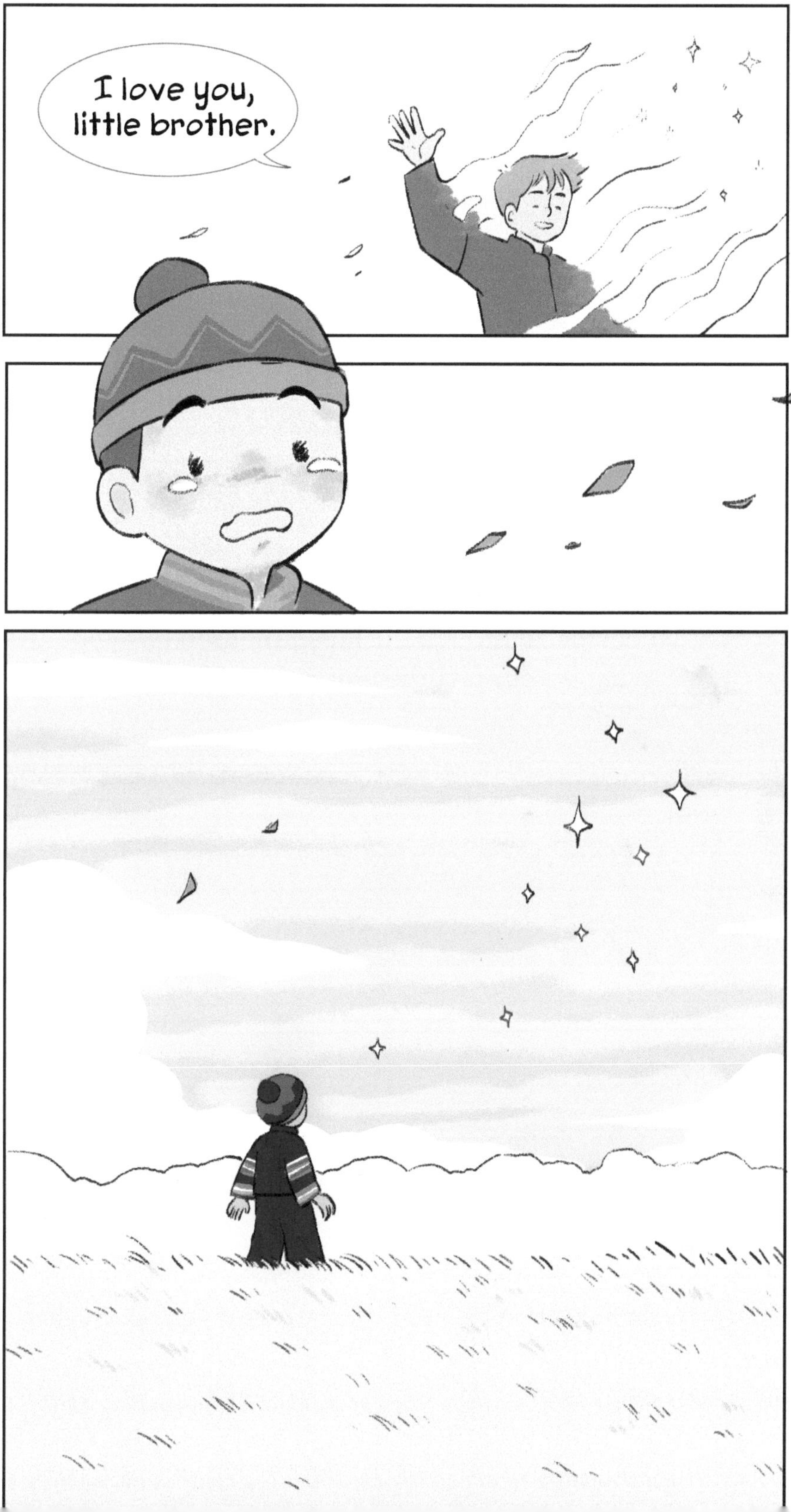
I love you, little brother.

WRITING PROMPTS

1. At the end of this story, Tou Dao says, "Something happened in the jungle." What do you believe happened? Use examples from the story to support your answer.

2. Discuss some of the ways the brothers helped each other in the story. Then talk about some of the ways your sibling or friend helps you.

3. Look back through the illustrations in this book. What is your favorite illustration and why?

DISCUSSION QUESTIONS

1. The Brothers is a Hmong folktale. Research more about the Hmong people, and then write down a few of the most interesting facts about this culture.

2. Folktales were often told aloud before they were ever written down. Think about a story your parents, teachers, or friends have told you in the past. Then try to write down that story from memory.

3. What happens next? Write a sequel, or second part, to this tale. You decide!

GLOSSARY

archer (AR-chur)—a person who shoots with a bow and arrow

game (GAYM)—animals pursued or taken by hunting

jerky (JUR-kee)—dried meat

navigate (NAV-uh-gayt)—to make one's way about over, or through

protected (pro-TEK-tuhd)—covered or shielded from something that would destroy or injure

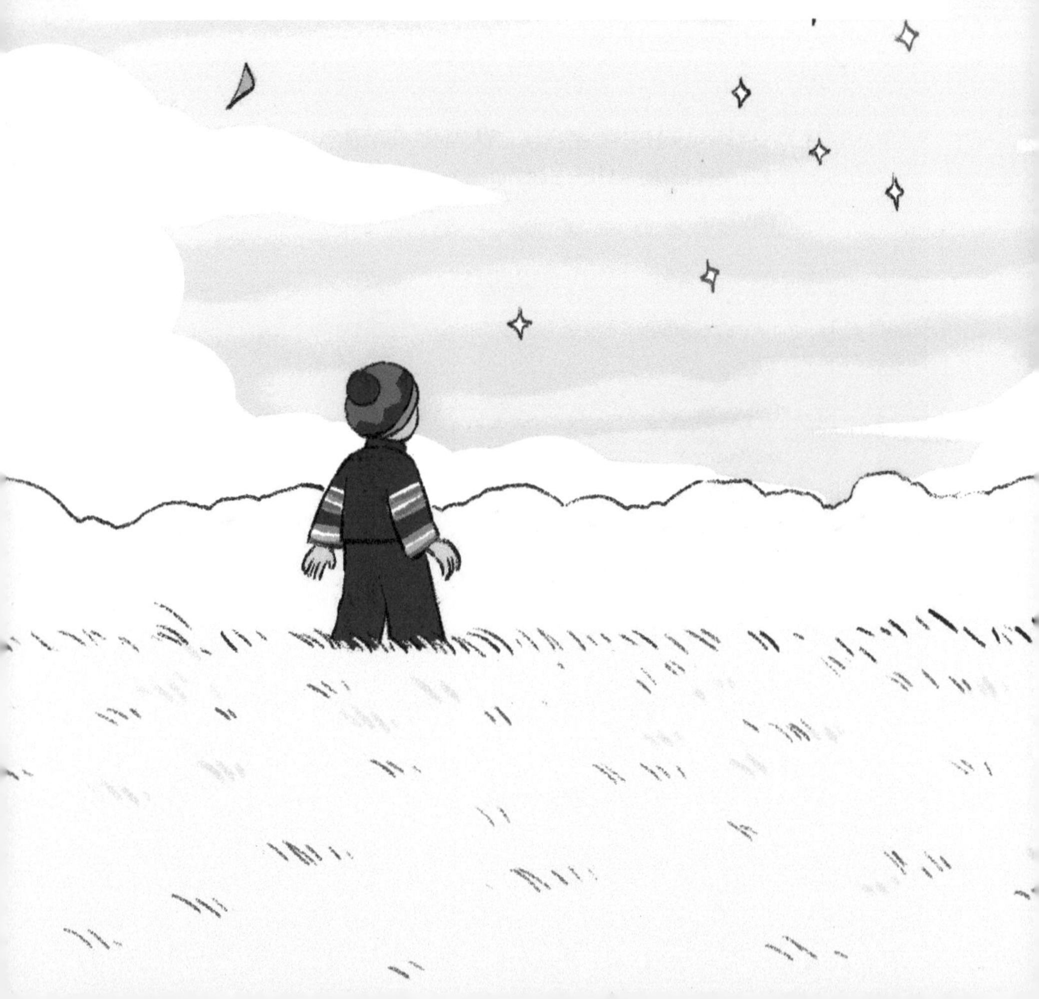

ABOUT THE AUTHOR

Sheelue Yang is an editor and writer based in east St. Paul, Minnesota.

ABOUT THE ILLUSTRATOR

Le Nhat Vu was born in Nha Trang City, a seaside city in Vietnam. While growing up there, he taught himself to draw by studying art documents and the works of other artists. He especially enjoyed reading manga (Japanese comics) and trying to draw the illustrations in his favorite comic books. Today, Nhat Vu works in Ho Chi Minh City, where he loves to watch and play football, read novels, watch movies, and listen to old pop music.

READ ALL THE
AMAZING
DISCOVER GRAPHICS BOOKS!